GEM C[...] 90
MANY WORDS

Gem likes Bec.

Bec can say words.

Bec, Bec, Bec.

Gem laughs.

Bec

Bec

Bec

4

Gem can say Bec, Bec, Bec.

Bec is happy.

Bec

Bec

Bec

6

Gem can say, Gem, Gem, Gem.

Bec can say, Gem, Gem, Gem.

Gem
Gem
Gem
Gem
Gem
Gem

8

Gem laughs.

Bec can stop in the garden.

Bec can say words to Gem and Tas.

Kid, kid, drag, drag, sled, sled, scat, scat.

kid

kid

drag

drag

sled

sled

scat

scat

12

Gem and Tas listen.

Bec can say more words.

Jot, trot, jot, trot, jab, jab, jet, jet.

Bec heard words on the long hot trip.

trot

jot

jot

trot

jab

jab

jet

jet

16

Gem likes the words.

Gem can say, trip, slab, jet, jot, clip, clop, clap, kid, nut.

clip trip slab

jet

jot

nut

kid

clop   clap

18

Tas and Bec hear the words.

Gem can say words and she can read words.